THE GLASS PEOPLE

Alan Kilpatrick

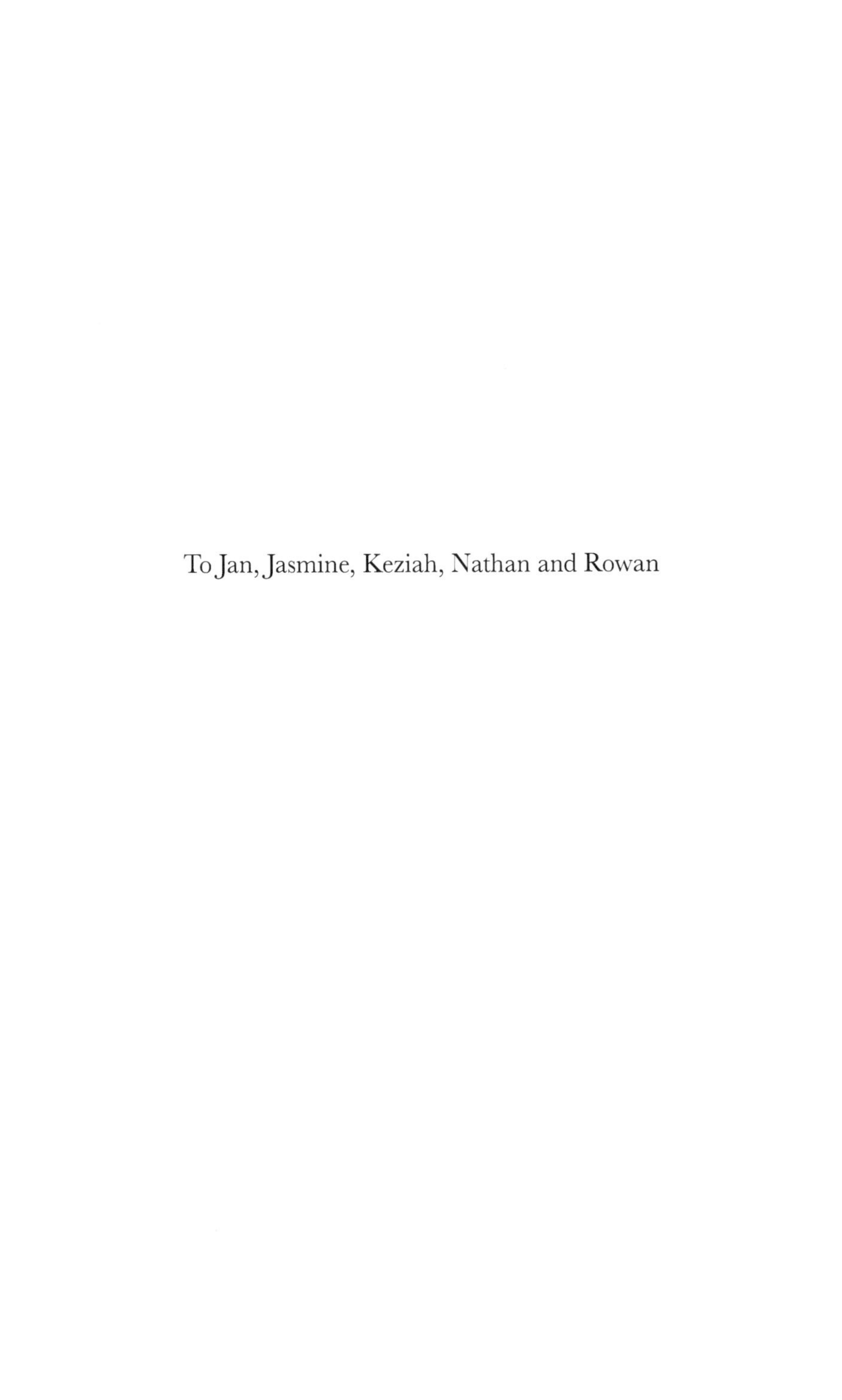

To Jan, Jasmine, Keziah, Nathan and Rowan

Jesus said,

'Whoever finds their life will lose it, and whoever loses their life for my sake will find it.'

Prologue

In a world full of glass the most frightening thing is a red-hot furnace. A furnace so hot that if any glass gets near it, the glass starts to melt. The furnace in the house on the hill was such a furnace. Large. Red-hot and bubbling. With steps into it and steps out of it. The furnace burned continually and the heat was intense. The furnace was in the home of the Glassmaker. He made everything out of glass and was continually tending the furnace. It was a beautiful house with many rooms and many doors. The house sat in the countryside on its own, with no other neighbours. Bird's flew between the eaves of the house and animals dwelt in peace in the gardens surrounding it. The sun shone and all was well. If we were high in the clouds we could zoom out and see what surrounds the garden and house. We would see mountains and rivers and a beautiful waterfall. Looking further away we would see a village - the village of Knock. The place where the heroes of our story live.

Chapter 1

The village of Knock lay at the bottom of a large hill. Trees covered the slopes of the hill, but at the top was a clearing where the hill stood higher than the tops of the trees and you could see all around the country. On the other side the village was bordered by a lake, a beautiful, blue lake - in fact it was called 'The Blue Lake' - not a very imaginative name, I know, but it was very blue! The blue lake was a wonderful place to fish. There were so many different types of fish - smackerel's, snout's, jumping jacks, belly face groupers (because their mouths looked like belly buttons!) and many, many more. All were tasty and lovely to eat. Day in and out fishermen would go into the lake to fish and return laden with lots of different types, birds following them hoping for a bite of lunch.

The quay, where the fishermen landed their catches, was full of activity - and very smelly, because of the fish. Dog's chased cats and fishwives shouted at their husbands for being out fishing too long. Children ran in between all of the adults, causing people to stumble and fall over into piles of smelly fish. People called out at market stalls trying to encourage others to come and buy their products. They shouted, 'Belly faced Groupers - two for a penny' or 'Three loaves of bread for a thrupence' or 'Apples - penny a bag'. It was very much like a chaotic village scene from a village in our world. Except for one important thing - everything was made of glass!

Chapter 2

Now this may seem very strange to us - a world made of glass - isn't glass dangerous? To us it is - so please be careful and don't ever play with real glass. But to the people of the glass world it was completely normal. They had glass sandwiches, ate glass apples and had glass beds. They caught glass fish in glass nets out of glass fishing boats. Everything was made of glass and it was completely normal to them. But if you looked closely at everything you noticed that they all had one thing in common (apart from being made of glass) - everything had cracks and chips. From the blades of grass to the people - everything was scratched and broken. Boats had cracks in the hulls. Men had one ear (the other had fallen off) and they always said 'Pardon!" Some birds had one wing and would fly around in circles. Some fishermen had nets with holes so big that they never caught any fish! This world had been created by the Glassmaker. It had been made perfect, but over time it had become chipped, cracked and broken. Even though they could people never went to the Glassmaker to be repaired because they were too afraid of him and most of them didn't really believe he was real anyway.

Chapter 3

In this broken village of Knock, inhabited by broken people, lived three children. They were called Daniel, Jonah and Ruth. Daniel was off average height, had dark hair and green eyes. Daniel was the one who was last when they were doing something naughty - not because he was a goody-two shoes but because he was scared. Jonah was the shortest of the three (and the roundest!). His nose kept falling off and he had to stick it to his face with tape. Jonah worried about everything. As we have said, Daniel would be the last one into doing something naughty, but Jonah would be the first to runaway after he had done something naughty as he'd be worried about being caught and not getting his pocket money. Ruth was always getting annoyed with the boys because she thought that their tricks and jokes were rubbish and that hers were much better. But the boys never listened to her - and that annoyed her.

As we enter the village the three friends running as fast as they can. Running to safety and away from the village policeman - Constable Bunce. He was cross! He had just walked into a room at the school and the three children had placed a bucket of cold water on top of the door that Constable Bunce had to go through to get into the room. The ice-cold water had fallen on top of him! The three children laughed and then they saw the angry stare of Constable Bunce and so they ran. The Constable, who was rather large and unfit, was trying to catch them. But he couldn't catch them and instead was huffing and wheezing. The children ran further away, laughing. They ran around a corner and Daniel hit the edge of the wall with his shoulder and chipped it.

'Oww!' he cried, as they continued running not able to pick up the small piece that had broken off.

'Oh my goodness we will get into such trouble' said Jonah.

'Keep running' cried Daniel, 'He still might be able to catch us.'

'Don't be such a scaredy cat, Daniel. There is no way that Constable Bunce can catch us now. It was a stupid idea anyway', said Ruth.

'No it wasn't', said Jonah (whose idea it was).

'Yes it was', cried Daniel and Ruth together, at which point they all burst out laughing again and slowed down and hid in an alleyway, until they were sure that Constable Bunce had stopped his pursuit.

Daniel examined his shoulder, which was cracked and painful. There was no hiding now that they had been up to mischief.

It was tea-time and the three had to go to their own homes - which they were not happy about as they were sure that their parents would have heard about their trick and be ready to tell them off.

Chapter 4

All of the houses were made of glass and they were very similar to an igloo. Thick blocks of cracked glass placed on top of each other until they met at the top. A hole was left in the roof to let smoke escape. Daniel walked to his family home, nervous of the welcome he would receive.

'Why do we do these things?', he thought to himself, regretting what they had done. 'But it was funny', he smiled to himself, holding his cracked shoulder.

He walked through the door of his home. The fire was burning in the middle and his family - mother Martha, father Peter and sister Sarah - were all standing waiting for him with Constable Bunce.

'Oh' said Daniel.

'Oh, indeed', replied his father.

'I'll be off now', said Constable Bunce, who put on his hat, walked to the door, looked sternly at Daniel and walked out.

Daniel kicked the floor and pursed his lips as his family looked at him in silence.

His father walked over to him.

'Have you anything to say for yourself?'

Daniel said nothing.

'What am I going to do with you?' his father's voice getting louder, ' you are on triple chores for the rest of your life! I will send you to the Glassmakers furnace if you keep doing this!'

At this point Daniel's mother saw his chipped shoulder and came quickly to his side.

She bent down beside him and started to fuss over his shoulder.

'Serves him right if he hurt himself', said his sister Sarah, who gave him a 'you're-in-trouble' smile.

'Leave him alone, Martha', said his father.

'Peter, he has hurt himself and it needs tending. He will do extra chores for a long time. Don't get so angry with him.'

Peter sighed, knowing his wife was right, and went to sit down beside the fire as Martha sorted Daniel's shoulder as best she could.

'I'm sorry Daniel for saying that I would send you to the Glassmaker's furnace. I was angry', said Peter as his children sat at his feet by the fire.

'Is there really a furnace, Daddy?', asked Sarah.

'People say there is. A huge, red-hot furnace that is ready to melt any glass'.

The children looked scared, eyes wide open and Daniel hid behind the seat.

Their father suddenly jumped out of his seat and makes a roaring sound. The children fell back on the floor in fear and then realised that their father was joking. Peter threw himself on the floor beside his children and started to tickle them and through the tickles Daniel thought, 'I truly love my family'.

'Is it real, though?', asked Daniel.

'No, it's just a myth'.

'But what about the house that we can see far away on the hill', said Daniel, 'Is that not the Glassmaker's house and isn't the furnace in there?'

In a world made of glass the scariest thing is a red hot furnace.

'Some people say that the house on the hill is the Glassmaker's house and that there is a furnace in it, but nobody knows for sure. If there is a Glassmaker, then why doesn't he come and help us?'

'Don't talk like that in front of the children', replied his wife.

'Why not?', said Peter, 'its true - if he made us and cares for us then why is he not here helping us?'.

'We could go to him', said Daniel.

As he said this everyone looked at him as though he had just said the silliest thing ever.

Chapter 5

The next day, after Daniel had finished triple chores, the three friends climbed through the forest on the hill to their favourite spot - the clearing at the top of the hill where they could see everything. As they climbed through the forest glass, squirrels scurried away and ran up the trees and bird's flew through the leaves, singing at the top of their voices. Daniel, Jonah and Ruth played hide and seek behind the trees trunks as they climbed closer to the clearing and talked about the upcoming thanksgiving celebration - the day when all families gathered together in the streets and celebrated summer.

'I cannot wait for Mrs Ferwinckle's cakes. They are the best', said Jonah.

'You are always thinking of your stomach', joked Daniel.

'No I am not. I just appreciate good baking!'

'Your large stomach shows your appreciation' said Ruth as she ran away from Jonah, who was now chasing her.

They eventually reached the top of the hill and entered into the clearing, where they all stood in silence looking into the distance. Daniel looked at the pin-prick of a house that people said was the Glassmakers home and wondered what the truth about the Glassmaker was.

'Oh, I cannot wait for the boar on the spit - that's always

the best part', Jonah was still talking about the food and the thanksgiving celebration. 'Do you remember last year', he continued, ' when the chair of grumpy Mr Crudge broke and he fell backwards into the bucket of chicken intestines?'

Daniel's attention was taken from the Glassmaker's house by Jonah's comment and they all sat on top of the clearing, laughing.

Sitting in silence and admiring the view, Daniel said, 'I love it here! Despite all the cracks and chips'.

The sun slowly rose, the colour changing from a deep red to yellow. They enjoyed its warmth and they lay back on the glass grass and were thankful.

After a few moments they all heard a strange sound. It sounded like the sound of someone shouting. The noise got louder, and Daniel, Jonah and Ruth all stood up and looked down at the village. Horrified, they saw that smoke was rising from the houses in Knock and that grey, glass men were riding around the village on horse back. The village was under attack.

Chapter 6

The children couldn't believe what they were seeing. The village had never been attacked before.

'No!', cried Daniel, as he started to run down to help, but stopped as he saw how many soldiers there were.

Jonah stared silently in disbelief, his mouth hanging open.

'We must do something - quickly', urged Ruth

'But, what? There are so many of the grey soldiers - on horses! There is no way we can help, no matter how badly we want to', replied Daniel, a tear running down his cheek.

'You're a coward!', accused Ruth.

Daniel didn't say anything - he just sighed and hung his head.

Jonah was still staring silently.

As he watched, grey soldiers on horseback and on foot went through the village laughing and smashing houses and sinking boats. People were running in every direction trying to escape. Constable Bunce was attempting to bring order but it was hopeless, and he was knocked to the ground by a passing rider.

'Who are these people?', Jonah asked, breaking his silence, tears running down his face.

Ruth had started to run down the hill towards the village.

'I don't know, but I am going to smash them to pieces!

Come on, let's go.'

She ran a little way down the hill before she realised that she was alone. She had expected the boys to follow. She was wrong. They stayed where they were, looking at their precious village and then at Ruth, ashamed because they were too scared.

'Boys are supposed to be brave!' shouted Ruth, furious that the boys hadn't followed her.

The noise of smashing glass stopped and Daniel, Ruth and Jonah watched in despair as they saw everyone in the village rounded up, tied up and lifted on to carts. Their whole village was being taken prisoner.

Chapter 7

Daniel shouted in anger, fear, loss and many other emotions, but his cry was unheard. He watched helplessly as he saw his family tied up and hauled onto a cart.

He sank to his knees, snot flowing freely. He could see his sister crying, his mother, whose face was full of fear, trying to comfort her.

The families of Ruth and Jonah were taken hostage too.

"We must go and help',said Ruth, tears running down her face, 'we have to rescue them. We are their only hope. We have to, we have to, we have to…'

'But there are too many of them, we would just get captured', said Jonah, ' and then how could we help them?'

'You're just scared', said Ruth.

'Yes I am scared', replied Jonah, 'But what I said is still true!'

In the clearing on top of the hill everything went quiet except for the occasional crash of glass as another house fell down. The village was empty. All their family and friends had been taken prisoner.

Suddenly Daniel noticed that some of the grey soldiers on horses were looking around them, as though they were looking for someone who they had missed. To the children's horror they started to ride through the forest, up the hill towards where they were.

'Run!' Ruth cried out.

At once all three of them started to run away from the village.

One of the difficulties with glass is that when it catches the light is can be like a lighthouse and tell everyone else where you are. That is exactly what happened. The riders saw the glint from the sun shining on the three children's glass bodies and they started to pursue them.

Unaware that they have been seen the children continued to run and run, bumping into rocks and hitting tree branches in their escape, and making more scratches and chips on their little glass bodies.

Daniel suddenly saw a cave in the side of the hill.

'Quick, over here. We can hide in this cave.'

The cave was dark and cold. Water dripped somewhere in the darkness.

The soldiers rode past the children's hiding place and the children breathed a sigh of relief that they were safe - for now.

They continued to stay quiet until they were sure that it was completely safe and that the rider's would not come back.

Ruth looked at Daniel who seemed to be deep in thought.

'What are you thinking about?'

'Nothing.'

'Yes you are - you have that look on your face that you have when you are trying to figure something out'

'I am not thinking about anything.'

'Daniel!', shouted Ruth and Jonah together.

After a moment Daniel lifted his eyes and looked at his two friends 'You're not going to like it! The only person that can help us is the Glassmaker. We have to go to his house!'

Chapter 8

'What!' said Ruth, 'Are you mad!'

'I can't believe you would even think that!' said Jonah ' What on earth are you thinking? We have to be realistic and try and work out some way to get our families back.'

'I am', replied Daniel. 'There's no way that we can do this by ourselves. We need help.'

At this Ruth grabbed Daniel and shook him.

'The Glassmaker is just a myth and even if he is real, why would he want to help us?'

Daniel pushed her away and stood breathing heavily.

'I am not sure about the Glassmaker, whether he is real or not or if he would even help us if we asked him, but for the sake of our families we have to try. There is no other way. I am terrified at the thought of going to the house on the hill, but the thought of my family suffering gives me a little bit of courage. I would do anything for my father and mother, and my sister.

'Wouldn't we all', said Jonah 'but your idea is insane!'

'Maybe, so what do you think we should do?'

Jonah had no idea of what to do and he stayed silent.

'If you don't want to come then fine, but I am going to try and get help.'

At this Daniel stood up and walked out of the cave into the

sunlight, checking to make sure that there were no soldiers lurking about.

Ruth and Jonah stood looking at each other.

'Better than doing nothing', Ruth said and followed Daniel out of the cave leaving Jonah alone.

'Wait for me!', Jonah cried, running after the other two.

Chapter 9

The sun was shining as the three friends walked gloomily along the barren road. They had gone back to the village after they had left the cave to gather supplies for their journey. The sight of what had once been their homes, smashed and broken, had filled them with sadness and dread and the sense that they just had to take this journey to the Glassmakers house, even if none of them really wanted to. They had to try and rescue their families.

By the time they had reached the farthest point any of them had been before they had been walking all day and were tired. Actually, no-one they knew had been this far because the people of Knock weren't great travellers. They all stopped and looked at each other. They held hands and took a step forward together. It wasn't long before the heat of the day and the length of the journey tired the children out.

'How far do you think we have to go before we reach the house?' said Jonah, too afraid to use the word Glassmaker.

'I really haven't the foggiest idea', said Ruth sarcastically, 'I've never been there before.'

'Just asking', replied Jonah and he slowed down and walked behind the other two.

'No need to be mean.', said Daniel, 'He's just saying what we are all thinking.'

'Well, I don't know and I don't want to know how long before we get there, as I'm not sure I really want to go there anyway', said Ruth who then strode on ahead also so they all walked separately.

They walked in this way for about half an hour until Jonah ran past them as fast as he could, shouting, 'Run! They're coming!'

Not quite sure who 'they' were, Daniel and Ruth stood still for a moment and turned around to see why Jonah was running. They very quickly started to run as well as they caught sight of four grey soldiers on horses riding quickly towards them.

Chapter 10

They weren't sure if the soldiers had seen them or not, so they ran as fast as they possibly could. Hope grew as they saw that they were running towards a forest. They all made for a path in the forest that they could see, and as soon as they were in the forest they left the path and hid in the roots of some enormous trees a short way from the path.

Desperate for air after running they hardly dared breathe, fearful that they would be heard by the passing soldiers. Eventually they heard the hooves of the horses as the riders moved into the forest and started down the path - which was difficult as the path was narrow and branches were at the same height as the riders' faces. After what seemed like an eternity Daniel, Ruth and Jonah could no longer hear the soldiers. The soldiers had left.

Darkness had started to fall and no one talked. Soon all three were fast asleep.

In the darkest part of the night an owl flew near the children. Daniel was awoken by the owl, but then he also heard the crunching of glass underfoot. His heart started to pound as he became fearful that the soldiers had turned back and were moving towards them. He sat up and looked around. All was silent again and he thought he must have dreamt it. He started to lay back down again when out of the corner of his eye he became aware of a growing light. It seemed to be far away, but as he looked he could see that it was getting brighter and closer.

Without saying a word he shook the other two. Annoyed that they had been disturbed they complained.

'Leave me alone', said Jonah who then turned over and tried to go back to sleep.

Daniel shook him again, 'Wake up!'

Ruth groggily sat up and looked at Daniel. He continued to stare at the light and so Ruth turned around to follow his gaze. She tensed as she saw the light, and she moved closer to Daniel.

Jonah groaned, 'Oh my goodness me, what is the problem - I am so tired and I…' but he never finished his sentence as he saw the light. which was getting closer, lighting up all the surrounding forest, and making the shadows of trees and roots move and flicker as it moved towards them. There was no way of getting away from this light, even if they wanted to. The children were surrounded by the light.

Chapter 11

The children shielded their eyes because the light was so bright. It was so bright in contrast to the darkness.

The light stopped moving and started to fade in intensity. As their eyes started to adjust to the light they began to see the outline of a figure. Amazed, and slightly terrified, they saw a beautiful person emerge out of the light. This person had no cracks, no scratches, he was perfect.

'Hello', said the figure, breaking the silence of the night.

The children just stared, not knowing what to do or how to respond.

'Hello', the figure said again, 'My name is Nathaniel. What are yours?'

Daniel, Ruth and Jonah looked at each other and Ruth was the first to speak.

'I'm Ruth.'

'Pleased to meet you.'

'I'm Daniel.'

'I'm Jonah and I'm a wee bit scared of you!'

'No need to be frightened', replied Nathaniel, 'I'm not here to harm you, but to help you'.

'What are you?' asked Daniel.

'I'm like you.'

Jonah laughed. 'You are nothing like us. You are beautiful!'

Nathaniel smiled. 'I am just like you. In fact, I am one of you. I was once scared, alone, cracked and chipped - but not anymore.'

'How is that possible?' said Ruth, doubting what Nathaniel had said.

'I met the Glassmaker and he changed everything. I know why you are running and I know where you want to go. Keep going and don't give up. There will be obstacles but you can overcome them. Stay on the right path. He is waiting for you. Remember His words:

When hands are grabbing for what they can get
Make sure you hold onto that which is best
You can climb the mountain when you see
That letting go will set you free
When stuck in the middle of that which is clear
Push on through and do not fear.'

By this time Nathaniel had started to fade away.

'Wait! Please stay! Is the Glassmaker real? What will happen when we get to the Glassmaker?'

But it was too late - the children were once again plunged into darkness.

Not sure what to say, they said nothing.

Chapter 12

The three had been confused by what had happened during the night and had eventually drifted off into an uneasy sleep, but all had awoken as soon as the sun started to rise.

"Did that really happen last night or was it a dream?' asked Daniel.

'If it was a dream then it was the most realistic dream I have ever had', stated Jonah, who had been disturbed by the night events the most.

'Whether it was real or not, what did he mean that there would be obstacles? If the Glassmaker wants to see us then why should it be difficult to see him - surely he would make it easy?' said Daniel.

Ruth had been quiet up till now sorting out some breakfast. 'Maybe he wants to see how much we really want to see him', she said.

'Why should he do that?' said Daniel, getting a little bit cross with the whole situation and a big bit frightened, 'I'm not even sure that I want to go to him if he is going to make it difficult to get to him - how silly!'

Jonah was looking at Ruth and then at Daniel as they both started to get frustrated with each other.

'Well, just go home then if you feel frightened', said Ruth, 'I am going to continue as I want to rescue my family even if you don't.'

Well this was the last straw and Daniel shouted at Ruth, 'How dare you say that! I want to rescue my family as much as you do'.

'Well prove it', Ruth replied, and she picked all of her stuff up and walked away from the other two.

Jonah looked at Daniel, picked his things up and then followed Ruth saying, "I'm going with her - she's scary!'

Daniel stood still, staring at the ground as his anger slowly went away. He was frustrated because he knew that Ruth was right - they did have to go on if they wanted to rescue their families. But he was scared.

'Come on Daniel', he said to himself, 'Just take the next step.'

With that he slowly followed the other two.

Chapter 13

They had been walking for several hours through a rocky, glass terrain that had made their journey a bit more difficult, when a little stream started to appear. They continued on in silence and slowly the stream started to grow bigger and bigger. The stream soon grew and became very big and very loud as the water rushed quickly past them.

They looked up and down the river realising that the river blocked their progress down the path they were following. They began to get worried as they could see no bridge or boat or any way to cross it.

'How are we going to get across? There's no way', said Jonah

'There must be a way', replied Ruth, but in her heart she was not so sure.

'We just have to go through it', said Daniel, surprising the other two with his brave words.

Daniel stepped gingerly in the edge of the water. The current was very strong, even at the edge. He took a few more steps and although the current was strong it only came up to his waist - even when he had made it into the middle.

'It's not deep, come on!' he cried to his companions.

Ruth and Jonah followed him and they were soon in the middle of the river with him.

Jonah said, 'This is going to be easy'.
But he said it all too soon.
They started to feel something grabbing their legs.

Chapter 14

Panic started to set in as they all tried to rush quickly to the other side of the river, but it soon became impossible.

They looked at the water in horror as they saw hands emerge from the water trying to pull them under. The whole river soon transformed into a mass of hands.

As much as they struggled, they could not get free. They desperately looked at one another and then at the shore.

'Help me!', shouted Jonah as he was pulled further down.

Daniel tried to get closer to him, but he too was pulled further down.

Then Ruth remembered the first two lines of the verse that Nathaniel had told them:

When hands are grabbing for what they can get

Make sure you hold onto that which is best

'We need to hold onto one another - we need each other', she shouted above the roar of the river.

Not quite understanding what she meant, but with no other idea, Daniel and Jonah stretched out and the three were just able to hold each other's hands.

As soon as they did that the horrible hands coming out of the water started to let go as though they had no grip.

Realising that escape was possible they all moved quickly

to the riverbank. It was still difficult, but as they got closer to the edge the river spat them out onto the ground as though it was fed up with trying to hold onto them.

They were safe.

Chapter 15

They tumbled over the rough ground, chipped and scratched a little bit more, but happy to be safe.

They looked back at the river but it was just a normal river now with flowing water. No sign of the hands.

Daniel started to laugh. He was not sure why, but he laughed louder and louder. Ruth and Jonah soon joined in and the three rolled on the ground, relieved that they were alive.

Suddenly Nathaniel appeared. Their laughter stopped and they all looked at him.

Ruth was the first to speak.

'What on earth were those hands? It was terrifying!'

Nathaniel replied, 'They were the hands of people who tried to cross the river without thinking of others. Life is about one another - helping, loving, serving. The only way you crossed the river was by holding each other's hands and helping one another. This meant that the hands in the river had no grip on you. Keep going'

And with that he disappeared.

Jonah said, 'I'm getting a bit fed up with him disappearing before we can ask him any more questions.'

At that Daniel and Ruth burst out laughing again.

Chapter 16

More chipped and broken than they had ever been before they continued to walk the path for another three days. The surroundings changed as they continued and soon they saw mountains in the distance - small at the moment, but getting bigger with every step they took.

Snow covered the top of the mountains and very soon they were towering over the three travellers.

'There is no way to get over these mountains', said Daniel as he bent backwards to try and see the top of the sheer walls of rock.

They walked along the base of the mountains, their desperation increasing.

'Over here,' shouted Jonah, who had found a dark gorge in the rockface.

When Daniel and Ruth arrived they saw that to enter the gorge they needed to be full of courage as it was very dark and narrow. They didn't have much of that at the moment, but their river crossing had given them a little bit of bravery.

They all knew that they had to continue, but were afraid to take the first step.

Eventually Daniel put out his hands for Ruth and Jonah to hold.

'Come on. If we learnt anything from the river it was that

we have to do this together.'

Ruth and Jonah took his hands and they walked into the deep, dark gorge.

Chapter 17

They were caught by surprise. They had expected to walk through the gorge in darkness, fumbling and feeling their way through. It had been like that for a short distance, but then in the darkness, they had felt cold flakes of something fall on their faces. Frightened that it was something terrible they started to run away in a panic. Then the darkness seemed to fade and they found themselves in a snow scene! Thick snowdrifts banked the sides of the gorge and the snow fell constantly. It was beautiful!

Jonah made a snowball and threw it at Daniel. It hit him on the back of the head, and after the initial shock he too made a snowball and threw it back, hitting Jonah. Soon a full scale snowball fight was in the progress, with the children running around, hiding behind rocks and whooping as they hit someone. They all ran at each other with snowballs flying and they slipped on some ice and collapsed in a heap laughing.

'We must get going', said Daniel, 'but only after we have made made a snowman.'

They trudged through the snow, happy and cold, when they encountered two paths. Which way should they go? Stay on the right path, Nathaniel had said, but which one was the right path?

'This is unfortunate!' said Ruth, whose teeth had started to chatter.

'It would be really good to have a map!', Jonah said

Three little red-breasted robins were flying around and they stopped on a leafless tree beside the beginning of the paths.

They looked at the children and seemed to be trying to speak to them.

'Are those robins trying to speak to us?' Ruth asked, really not believing that they were.

'Don't be silly - birds don't speak, they chirp or tweet', replied Daniel

'But they really do look like they are trying to speak to us', insisted Ruth

The birds suddenly took flight and flew in circles around the beginning of one of the paths.

'Do you think they are trying to show us the way?', said Daniel

'Or the wrong way!' said Jonah

'I don't think so', said Daniel who had started to follow the path the birds had pointed out.

Jonah followed, grumbling, 'Since when do birds speak and show us the way!'

Chapter 18

When it became clear to the robins that the children had followed them on to the right path - for they were good robins and as we shall see the closer you got to the Glassmaker the more magical things became - they flew away.

'Thank you little birds', shouted Daniel

'Lucky guess', said Jonah, still not sure they were actually on the right path, 'Robins are rascals'.

'No, you're the rascal - Robins are sweet.'

'No, I am sweet and the robins are rascals!'

Ruth was about to reply when Daniel said, 'Stop bickering. Look the snow is getting deeper'.

And it was true. The snow was falling more heavily and it was definitely getting deeper. It made it so much harder to walk, especially since they had backpacks, filled with food and clothes and tools.

'This is hard work!', said Ruth

'Yes - especially since you filled your backpack with clothes and dresses!' replied Jonah.

Ruth just glared at him.

They trudged on through the thick snow.

'I wish I was a robin - at least I could fly over this snow', said Jonah.

The Glass People

The snow was so heavy now they could barely see in front of them. Suddenly they all banged into a wall, a wall of ice.

'Ouch', said Jonah, who was picking up his nose, which had fallen off again.

The wall was immense and high. Through the falling snow they could just about see the top, with the three robins perched on it.

'Show offs!', yelled Jonah

On the wall of ice there were bits of ice jutting out.

'I wonder if we could climb up using those bits of ice as foot holds', wondered Daniel

'Those aren't bits of ice', said Ruth, whose voice was shaky, 'They are people!'

Chapter 19

The children were horrified as they looked up the sheer face of the wall of ice. They staggered backwards and fell onto the cold ground.

As they were looking up they saw a figure at the top alongside the robins - it was Nathaniel!

He floated down from the top of the wall and was soon standing beside the children.

Still shaken by the sight of the frozen people stuck to the wall they stood up and looked at Nathaniel.

He smiled at them.

'You're wondering who these unfortunate people are'.

They all nodded.

'Like the people who were captured by the river, these are people who were on the same journey as you, but they have been stuck to the wall'.

Ruth was looking at the frozen people.

'Why didn't they make it? Why didn't they get to the top? Why did they get stuck?'

Ruth had so many questions.

'The people tried to climb this wall with everything they had brought with them. They attempted to climb with their backpacks, pots, pans, clothes, food, money, but all of that was too heavy and they took too long to climb, and so they were frozen to the wall'.

The children were visibly shaken by what he said.

Nathaniel continued, 'If you want to get over this wall then you have to leave everything behind. Everything'.

This was a frightening thought. Leave everything. How would they survive? What would they eat?

Knowing their thoughts Nathaniel said, 'Don't worry about anything. Do you not remember what I said to you:

You can climb the mountain when you see

That letting go will set you free'.

The children looked at each other.

Daniel was the first to speak, 'We have no choice. We've come this far, we can't turn back', and with that he threw all his belongings to the ground.

The strangest thing happened. Daniel started to float. He got higher and higher and was nearly at the top of the wall when the other two quickly threw off their belongings and they too started to float!

Chapter 20

They floated past all of the people who had tried to hold onto to their belongings, but had got stuck on the wall. It was a horrible sight. They were all so glad to reach the top of the wall and even more so when they had stopped floating and landed on the ground.

They smiled at one another and couldn't quite believe what had just happened.

The robins were still at the top of the wall and were flying around them. One of them landed on Jonah's shoulder and promptly started to talk!

'Welcome, welcome, welcome!' it said, 'We are so glad you made it. It has been such a long time since anyone has'.

Jonah was so surprised that he fell to the ground again.

The birds chirped all the more at that and Jonah thought they were laughing at him. Nathaniel had floated up the wall as well and was laughing at Jonah, but he didn't stop at the top he kept on floating until he disappeared from sight.

'I've never heard an animal talk before', said Daniel.

'None of us have. It's amazing!', said Jonah.

One of the robins landed on Ruth's head.

'The closer you get to the Glassmaker the more magical it becomes.', the bird tweeted.

'Will there be more amazing things?', asked Ruth

'So much more', the bird replied, 'But for now you must keep going. Slide down this slope and it will lead you to the path you must follow.'

The children thanked the birds for helping them and as they flew off, the three friends slid down the icy slope - it was scary and exciting at the same time. They could see the end of the gorge as it was getting lighter and lighter and soon they were thrown out of the dark gorge into bright sunshine.

Chapter 21

The children lay enjoying the warmth of the sun after the coldness of the dark gorge.

The grass was soft and birds and insects flew around their heads. It was wonderful to relax after their last adventure.

When they had left all of their backpacks behind at the foot of the ice wall they had been worried about what they would eat as all of their food had been in the bags. But now they saw that they need not have worried at all. There were fruit trees growing in this land. Fruits with amazing flowers, and of different varieties and size. They ran around the trees picking up different types of fruit and eating them, encouraging each other to try the fruit they had just eaten. It was so sweet, so juicy, so filling.

It wasn't long before the children needed another nap because they had eaten so much.

They were lying in the grass in the warm sun when suddenly Daniel sat up abruptly.

'Did you see that?', he said with a trembling voice, pointing to the sky above.

'See what?', said Ruth, straining her eyes to try and see what Daniel had seen.

After a moment she also saw it - a huge, winged monster flying through the air, moving quickly this way and that way as though it was being chased. But who on earth or what would that monster be frightened off?

'Quickly - hide!'

They quickly moved to find cover in case the monster saw them and attacked them. Hearts racing they followed the movements of the creature from their hiding place and then, suddenly, the monster stopped flying and started to fall as though it had been injured. It then disappeared from sight altogether.

Daniel, Ruth and Jonah didn't wait to discuss what they had just seen - they started to run towards the Glassmaker's house!

Chapter 22

Completely confused by what they had just seen, the children ran towards a forest that they had spotted in the distance.

'Let's hide in the forest', cried Daniel.

They stopped on the edge of the forest, unsure whether they should go in, as the place they thought would give them safety now looked very scary close-up.

'I'm not going in there', said Jonah backing away from the enormous trees.

'Where are you going to go? You can't go back - there's nothing there and you don't know what else is going on in the sky that we can't see', replied Ruth staring at the forest.

Jonah looked up into the sky and recalled the enormous flying monster that they had seen. He sighed, knowing that Ruth was right. They had to go into the forest. They had to get to the Glassmaker.

'What's going to happen to us in here?' asked Jonah walking into the forest.

It was hard work. The trees were gigantic with huge roots coming out of the ground that were covered with a deep green slippy moss. The children had to scramble over the slippery roots and were constantly hurting their knees and shins.

Even so, the children's determination to get through the

forest and into the Glassmaker's house was growing. They were becoming more and more confident and their fear was getting less and less. They had overcome two obstacles - together and with some help. Whatever they now faced they all started to believe that they could finish the journey. At this point they had forgotten about the roaring furnace!

The noise of animals and birds was getting quieter, but another noise was growing. As they continued through the forest it got louder.

Soon they came upon the source of the noise. An enormous waterfall, crashing down onto the rocks below. On either side were trees. They were so big you couldn't see the top of them. There was no way round the wall of trees and no way to climb them as the bottom of the trees had no branches to climb up.

However, through the waterfall they could see another land, a garden that was always changing in the flow of the water. They could see the blurred outline of the Glassmaker's house and they realised that they were nearly at their goal. The only way that they could see to get there was to go through the waterfall!

Chapter 23

Suddenly they heard shouts from the forest. The enemy soldiers had not stopped looking and somehow had discovered the children. They were in danger.

With the memory of the flying monster still fresh, and the shouts of the enemy soldiers nearby, they all ran towards the waterfall, knowing this was their only option.

Daniel picked up a stone and threw it into the cascading water. The stone entered the water and then simply hung in the water, moving down very slowly to the ground. Ruth picked up another stone and threw it into the water and did the same. This time the stone was spat out of the water and hit Jonah on the nose, who yelled in pain.

'Sorry Jonah', said Ruth, eyes still fixed on the water.

Daniel said, 'What shall we do?'

Jonah said nothing. He stepped forward and walked into the waterfall.

Chapter 24

Time stood still for Jonah - or that's what it felt like to him. He could hardly move. It was like being stuck in a jar of treacle (not that I have ever been stuck in a jar of treacle!). He could see the others outside and then he saw the soldiers emerge from the trees - they were all moving so fast compared to him. He started to panic and tried to wriggle through. He could move, but ever so slowly. Not only was it difficult to move but the water was pressing him into the ground and he was finding it difficult to breathe. He pushed on.

By this time the other two had entered the water and they too were moving slowly through towards Jonah. They were having real difficulty breathing and their hearts were pounding as their bodies cried out for air.

They were close enough to each other to hold hands when they heard the splash of the soldiers as they entered the waterfall. They were so close to the three children, but they were also having trouble moving and breathing.

Jonah was nearly out of breath now but he was nearly at the other side of the waterfall. He was almost fainting. He closed his eyes and thought of his family, tied up and taken hostage by an unknown enemy. He remembered what Nathaniel had said,

'When stuck in the middle of that which is clear
Push on through and do not fear'

The picture of those he loved suffering, and the encouragement of Nathaniel, gave him the extra bit of strength that he needed and he pushed one last time, knowing that it would be his last push if he didn't get clear from the water.

Jonah suddenly disappeared. Ruth and Daniel soon followed him, all three landing flat out on beautiful long green grass. They all quickly got to their knees to see if the soldiers were coming. After a few minutes they relaxed. The soldiers must have turned back. They sat down and looked around and were confronted with the most beautiful garden they had ever seen.

Chapter 25

It took their breathe away. There were colours of the richest blues, greens and reds the deepest purples and brightest yellows. It almost blinded them. Then there was the fruit. Fruit they recognised and fruit they had never seen before. Huge apples. Enormous oranges. Massive grapes. Not to mention the flowers. Daisies taller than the children, in multiple colours, swaying in the breeze. The strange thing was that they seemed to follow the children, looking at them and smiling. Scented roses with no thorns filled the air with heady fragrances.

Daniel cried out, 'Duck, quickly', as a massive winged insect flew by. The children were convinced that it said 'Good morning' to them.

'Did you hear that?', said Ruth

Puzzled, Daniel was scratching his head, 'No it couldn't be. Insects don't talk'.

'Excuse us', came a voice from the ground. They looked down and saw a line of ants that were being blocked from going forward by Jonah's foot.

'Oh, sorry', said Jonah, who then said, 'Argh, did I just apologise to ants?'

They looked at one another, unsure at what this all meant. They remembered the saying, 'The closer you get to the

Glassmaker the more magical things become', but talking ants!?

'Have you noticed something else?' said Ruth.

'What?' said Daniel watching as the line of ants disappeared into the distance.

'Nothing in this garden is scratched or broken or chipped. Everything is perfect'.

'No, it can't be', said Jonah but as he spoke the words his eyes told him that it was true. Everything in the garden was perfect.

Chapter 26

As the children realised that everything in the garden was good and perfect, they had become more aware of how broken and dirty they were themselves. They hadn't realised just how scratched they had become until they stood beside the perfect flowers and fruit. It made them sad, but they also realised that the only one that could help was the Glassmaker, and so they continued on towards the house which was closer than ever - they would reach it very soon.

Daniel was picking some fruit off a tree when something caught his eye around the other side of the tree trunk. It was a foot in the grass. No - it was a whole person. Several people. Terrified, he stumbled backwards and cried out.

'Quick, over here.'

Ruth and Jonah came running to see what was wrong. Daniel just stood there pointing at the bodies lying on the ground.

'Are they d..d.dead?' said Jonah, eyes wide open.

'I'm not sure', said Daniel, his voiced trembling

'Hello', called Ruth.

'Shh', shouted the other two

Ruth ignored them. 'Hello' she called again.

There was no answer. Ruth took a step towards the bodies.

'Ruth, don't..', said Jonah, running to hide behind a tree

trunk.

Ruth continued. She reached the group of bodies on the ground and quietly knelt down beside one.

'They're only sleeping', and she shook one to try and wake them. But there was no response. She tried another person. Again, no response.

'What's wrong with them?' asked Daniel who had worked up the courage to come closer'.

'I don't know. They are in the deepest sleep that I have seen anyone in.'

'I must confess that I am getting a bit tired', said Jonah, wandering nervously up behind the other two.

A noise in the distance distracted them from the sleeping people.

'Soldiers', shouted Daniel, 'Run!'.

Chapter 27

Panic set in as they saw that the soldiers had come through the waterfall. Initially the children ran in different directions as the soldiers chased them, but eventually they all ended up running in the same direction, bumping into tree trunks, tripping over sleeping people and slipping in the grass.

Even though they had not run very far they soon began to feel very drowsy. Their vision started to blur and they couldn't focus on where they were going.

'Whats happening to us?' cried Daniel.

'I don't know', said Jonah in a sleepy kind of way, his speech slurring as he was getting too tired to speak.

Ruth could see the soldiers gaining ground. 'Keep going! They are going to catch us if we stop'. But she too was finding it difficult to keep running.

'It feels like someone has attached weights to my legs. I can hardly move', said Daniel, falling to his knees yawning, 'I'm so tired'.

'Don't..', yelled Ruth but she was of no help as she was sitting on the ground lying against a tree trunk and rubbing her eyes, 'Got to keep…'.

But it was too late. All three of them were in the deepest of sleeps as more soldiers burst through the waterfall.

This was when the animals came to help.

Chapter 28

Three horses appeared, one beside each of the children and knelt down beside them. Other animals gathered around them as though in a protective circle.

'Wake up!', yelled a monkey, as he shook the children.

'Try again', suggested a nearby pig, 'You didn't shake them hard enough'.

'Alright, alright', said the monkey, who was called Albert, and he shook them again.

Slowly the children started to wake up, but they thought they were still dreaming when they saw that a monkey was waking them up.

'You're in my dream', said Jonah to the other two and then looking at the monkey said, 'Hello nice baboon!'.

The monkey was very cross.

'No, you're in my dream' said Daniel, 'and it's not a baboon but an orang-utang'.

By this time the monkey was furious and all the other animals were shaking with laughter.

'Well, that's funny because I thought you were all in my dream', said Ruth.

'Im not a baboon or an orang-utang. I'm a chimpanzee, if you don't mind', said Albert.

This woke the children up very quickly as they all realised

that they were not dreaming but very much awake.

Looking out from behind the tree trunk where they had hidden, Daniel said, 'Don't hurt us!'

'I, we..', said Albert looking round at the other animals, 'we are here to help you. Don't be afraid'.

'Hurry, hurry', called some woodpeckers, who were flying and acting as lookouts, 'they are coming'.

'Get on the horses and ride away from here as fast as you can. Get to the Glassmaker's - he can help', said Albert, and with that warning the children clambered onto the still kneeling horses which then stood up and galloped off at speed.

'This is the strangest day I have ever had!', said Daniel.

'I know what you mean', replied his horse.

Ruth looked at Daniel and, despite the soldiers still chasing them, they laughed.

Jonah looked backward on his horse, 'I don't know why you are laughing - soldiers are trying to..'. He stopped talking as his horse slowed up.

The soldiers were all falling to their knees. What happened to the children started to happen to the soldiers. Soon they were all asleep on the ground.

Relieved, they got off their horses and said thank you to them, to which the horses replied that it was their pleasure and they trotted away.

Still not used to the idea of animals speaking, the children looked at one another and then turned around to continue their journey, but they found they were already there.

They were standing in front of the Glassmaker's house.

Chapter 29

They stopped laughing very quickly as they were confronted by a huge house. This was the Glassmaker's house and now they were here they weren't very sure that they wanted to go in.

It wasn't that the cottage was frightening, or even very impressive. It was that it was the Glassmaker's house and inside there was a furnace and they were closer to the burning, hot furnace than they had ever been before.

The cottage was small and made of irregular shaped stone. It had a thatched roof and two windows painted blue and a wooden door, also painted blue. There was a short path to the front door, with green bushes and tulips on either side.

The children looked at each other and then back at the house, they moved around nervously, wondering what to do next.

Doubts started to a creep in.

'I'm not sure that this was such a good idea', said Jonah, 'Everything around here is just so strange. What if all this is a show, so that the Glassmaker can throw people into his furnace?'

Ruth said nothing as she was also scared and wondering if they should have come.

Daniel looked at them both.

'Listen, I am scared and I don't know if this is right or not but we have come so far. The river of hands, the dark gorge, the waterfall. Remember Nathaniel and how he helped us. Even the animals helped us'.

'But what if they are all in the Glassmaker's plan to throw us into the furnace', interrupted

Jonah.

'Well if it is a conspiracy, it's a conspiracy of kindness and help', said Daniel.

As Daniel said this, the front door opened up by itself.

Chapter 30

The three of them stood still and were too afraid to go in. Although the door was open, the inside looked dark and frightening. They were unsure what to do. They had come so far, but they were scared. They stood looking at each other. Daniel was the first one to move. He turned towards the door and walked slowly to it.

'Daniel are you sure?', implored Jonah, who out of the three was now the least convinced that this was a good idea. In fact at that moment he would have happily started the journey home.

Daniel let out a sigh, 'Yes, we have to. I am scared, but so are our families. At least we are not prisoners. I miss them and that feeling is stronger than any fear I am feeling.' With that he continued walking through the door and disappeared from their sight.

Ruth and Jonah soon followed him into the darkness of the entrance. It took a few minutes for their eyes to adjust but when they had they found themselves in a gigantic hallway. Jonah ran out of the house again because he couldn't believe that such a big hallway could fit in the small house they had just walked into. He ran back in again.

'This is impossible. There is no way that this hallway could fit inside the cottage outside.'

Ruth reminded him what Nathaniel had said. The closer you get to the Glassmaker the more magical it became.

'I suppose it's possible. After all we have just talked to a monkey!' he replied.

'If that's true', said Daniel ,' then this must be the most magical place in the world'.

Chapter 31

They saw that there were lots of doors going off from the enormous hallway. They went to a few of them and saw that each door had a name above it. Names such as the 'Connected Kingdom', the 'Dark World', and the 'Ice Age'. Daniel pushed the door of the one with the name 'Connected Kingdom' on it.

'Don't' said Jonah.

But it was too late. Nothing horrible happened. The opposite in fact. They saw a beautifully colourful land with many villages and many people of different colours. From the doorway they were standing at a river of crystal clear water flowed into each of the villages. They went to a door with the words 'Dark World' over the top but there was no handle on the door to open it.

'I'm glad there is no handle. I don't think I want to look at a place called the 'Dark World', said Ruth.

They continued to explore the great hallway until they all became aware that someone, or something, was standing behind them. They were not alone.

Their hearts were pounding and they were too nervous to move. For what seemed like an eternity, but was probably only a few seconds, nothing happened. Ruth was the first to move. She slowly turned around and screamed. What she saw was a very large person with a horrible face that had no mouth or nose at all, and he was holding a big stick. She ran as fast as she could to the door. Daniel and Jonah turned around, screamed and ran for the door as well.

'Wait. I'm so sorry, but I forgot to take my protective mask off, said the person, who was, of course, the Glassmaker. But they kept on running.

'Daniel, Ruth, Jonah, wait. Don't be afraid', said the Glassmaker,' I am so glad you have come'.

When the glassmaker called them by name then the situation didn't seem quite so frightening. They all stopped and slowly turned around to look at the glassmaker who had now taken off his mask.

A wonderful head of white hair fell over his shoulders and a smile so wonderful that they felt instantly at ease.

'Welcome home' said the Glassmaker.

Chapter 32

Once again, the Glassmaker reassured them.

'Don't be afraid. I will not harm you. Why should I? I made you. But you have forgotten me, and you have lived without me. I was so ready to help you, but you didn't ask. Now all of my beautiful people are broken and chipped'

The children stood in silence not sure what to say. They had heard about the Glassmaker as the creator, but they thought it was just a myth, a nice story. But now they were confronted with the fact that it was true, and that truth was quite overwhelming.

'You know my name', said Daniel.

'Yes. And I know that you are brave and kind and generous.'

'I don't feel brave or kind or generous', replied Daniel

'That's because you have forgotten; all of the things that your have been through in your life have robbed you of your identity.'

'What about our families? They are hostages and in danger. We don't know who has taken them or where they have been taken. We didn't know what to do and in desperation we came to you. Will you help us?', asked Daniel, whilst the other two remained silent, listening to every word that was being said.

For a moment the Glassmaker said nothing and the children thought he was preparing to say no.

'Of course I will help you to help them - you are my answer to their need', he eventually said

'What do you mean help us to help them? What do you mean that we are their answer? We need you to go and do it. We are all chipped and broken. We can do nothing', said Jonah, getting a bit frustrated with the Glassmaker.

The Glassmaker just smiled. Jonah found that very annoying.

'I will remake you. I will make you strong and whole.'

'How is that possible?' asked Ruth, a bit more aggressively than she had intended.

The Glassmaker calmly replied, 'By walking through the furnace.'

Chapter 33

Jonah screamed. It was a really high pitched screamed and he was a bit embarrassed by it because it was not a very manly scream. The others looked at him.

'We have to leave NOW. Didn't you hear what he said? There is a furnace in this place and he wants to melt us down. I knew he wouldn't be good. We can rescue our families by ourselves', said Jonah in a breathless voice.

'Don't be so silly', said Ruth, angry at what Jonah was saying. She was scared at what she had heard, but she didn't want to go back.

'I'm not being silly', replied Jonah and the two of them argued for a few minutes. Meanwhile Daniel had said nothing. He was deep in thought.

'I'm scared', he thought to himself, 'but what about my family. I can't abandon them because that's what will happen if we try to rescue them by ourselves. We have no chance against whoever took them. But I don't want to go through a furnace. I don't want to be melted down. What do I do?'

The Glassmaker looked kindly on Daniel, as though he knew what he was thinking - which he did because he was the Glassmaker. Daniel looked up and saw the Glassmaker staring at him.

'Okay. I'll do it', said Daniel.

Ruth and Jonah stopped arguing and looked at Daniel, amazed at what he had just said.

Chapter 34

Jonah stared at Daniel, his eyebrows pushing together in disbelief.

'Are you mad?', he said, ' I thought the furnace was a joke to frighten people but now we find out it's real and you want to walk into it just because this man who we have just met asks you to? You're an idiot Daniel'.

The room was still and nobody moved after these words. Daniel and Ruth didn't move because they were embarrassed by what Jonah had said. Jonah didn't move because the words had come out more aggressively than he had intended, and he became more aware than ever of the towering presence of the Glassmaker.

The Glassmaker eventually broke the silence.

'Who do you think the shining ones are? Like Nathaniel whom you met on the road and who helped you', he asked.

They had no answer for him.

He continued,' They were people like you, who were broken and chipped and came to me because they needed help. They went through the furnace and now they are helping others and directing people to me. They were prepared to pay the cost to be made new again.'

Jonah felt very small and afraid and moved away from the Glassmaker, even though he had not been threatened in any way.

Daniel moved towards the Glassmaker.

'What do I do?' Daniel said to the Glassmaker

The Glassmaker said nothing but simply looked at a door. Above the door were two words: 'New Beginning'

Daniel moved towards the door.

Jonah shook his head and tried to stop him.

'What are you doing? You'll die and then how will you be able to help your family? He's just tricking you!'

Jonah couldn't look at the Glassmaker.

Ruth stared at Jonah.

'But what if he is telling the truth? It would change everything', and with that she walk towards Daniel.

Jonah stepped back from his friends, tears streaming down his face.

'I can't', he mumbled

He looked at the Glassmaker, and then back at his friends, and then he turned his back and walked out of the house.

Chapter 35

Daniel and Ruth were so sad that Jonah had left.

'What will you do?' asked the Glassmaker

They said nothing, but continued towards the door.

'Together', said Daniel

'Together', said Ruth as they turned the handle and pushed the door open.

The heat that hit them was unbearable and they felt terribly afraid.

They looked at the Glassmaker, and he walked over to them and put his hands on their shoulders.

'Don't be afraid. I will be with you.'

They turned to look at the furnace, which was glowing red and orange with smoke rising from it.

Their little bodies had started to glow red because the heat was so intense, but the presence of the Glassmaker gave them courage, and so they continued despite being afraid.

They moved closer and their bodies started to glow white as they got hotter and their bodies dripped onto the ground as they started to melt. Their hearts felt as though they would explode out of their chests.

By this time, the Glassmaker had walked around to the other side of the furnace. He seemed to be unaffected by the heat.

'Just look at me', he said as they stopped in fear.

It gave them both courage to see him across the furnace and they started to walk again towards it. In all their fear a confidence started to grow. It was very strange, but they started to feel a little bit of joy. They looked at each other bewildered.

They had been holding hands and by this time their hands had melted into each other's. And still the joy grew. There was no turning back.

They were on the steps now, walking down, eyes still fixed on the Glassmaker. Their legs started to melt and they slowly fell together into the furnace.

The last thing they saw was the smiling face of the Glassmaker.

Chapter 36

I know that this will be terrifying to hear, but very soon there was nothing left of the two children. They had been completely melted away. But the marvellous thing is that they were still there! Even though they didn't have bodies they still existed. What made them Daniel and Ruth was still there.

They discovered that all of their fear had gone. They felt utterly peaceful, rested and safe even though they had no bodies. It was a very strange situation, but it was also a very beautiful one.

They were not quite sure what had happened or what was happening. It felt to them that they were flying even though they had no body. They laughed even though they had no mouths and they looked at each other even though they had no eyes.

'Is this it?', thought Daniel.

Ruth replied by thinking, 'No, this is just the beginning'.

They could hear each other's thoughts! They laughed again in wonder. However this time as they laughed a mouth started to form. They could feel it. Their faces started to take shape and their bodies started to be created.

Then they felt themselves start to walk out of the furnace towards the smiling face of the Glassmaker.

Chapter 37

They had never felt so alive before. They both ran up to the Glassmaker and embraced him. In fact they ran so fast that they knocked him over and all three rolled on the floor laughing.

Then Daniel felt an urge that he had never felt before. He felt an urge to dance and he jumped to his feet and pulled Ruth up. They held hands and they spun round and round with the Glassmaker. Breathless, the Glassmaker invited them to look at the mirror. They looked in disbelief. They had no cracks or chips. They were perfect and they were both shining ones!

Speechless, they just looked at the mirror and then the Glassmaker and then back again to the mirror.

Eventually, Daniel found some words to say.

'In a world made of glass a furnace is not the most frightening thing. A furnace is a place of hope where things can be made new.'

Daniel remembered his family. This time he did not feel helpless. He felt powerful.

He looked at Ruth, 'We must go and rescue our families.'

Ruth agreed.

They both embraced the glassmaker.

* * *

At this time Jonah was walking through the garden. He was getting more and more cross as he was scared, alone and felt that his friends had abandoned him. And he was angry with himself for leaving his friends.

'I must make up for leaving my friends alone with that strange furnace man', and with that thought he started to wake up the sleeping soldiers.

Chapter 38

Daniel and Ruth walked to the door that led out of the house. They looked at the Glassmaker one more time and walked through the door together. As they got outside they gasped, as they saw a huge battle going on. Shining ones, flying monsters and soldiers chasing one another and fighting each other in the air and on the ground.

The Glassmaker came and stood beside them watching them and then looking at the on-going battle.

Daniel looked at the Glassmaker.

'What is happening here?', he asked, 'What is this?'

They all stepped back as an enormous flying monster flew by, with several shining ones chasing it.

'This is the unseen battle that has been going for many years. The shattered lord has been trying to break glass people.'

'What must we do?' asked Ruth as she watched the battle.

The Glassmaker looked at them both with great love.

'That's up to you', he said, 'You can go and build a nice house somewhere and settle down. Or you can fight'.

The Glassmaker didn't look at them but stared in the distance.

Daniel and Ruth looked at each other, knowing the answer, but nervous.

'We will fight.'

The Glassmaker smiled.

'I will always be with you. I will never leave you.'

Daniel was just about to reply to the Glassmaker when a shining one, who had been in the midst of the battle that had always been going on ran up to them and said, 'Come and fight for the glory of the Glassmaker'.

TO BE CONTINUED IN
'THE GLASS PEOPLE AND THE GREAT RESCUE'

About Alan Kilpatrick

Alan is married to Jan and they have four children. Alan is a Church of England priest and has led churches, with Jan, for over 21 years. In July 2017 they took a step of faith and stopped leading churches to move into mission work with Iris Ministries in Pemba, Mozambique. He is currently writing the next stories in The Glass People Trilogy and is planning to write other children's stories.

To contact Alan - alanwkilpatrick@icloud.com

Printed in Great Britain
by Amazon